In the Town

For Maia

OXFORD
UNIVERSITY PRESS

Great Clarendon Street, Oxford OX2 6DP.
United Kingdom

Oxford University Press is a department of the University of Oxford.
It furthers the University's objective of excellence in research, scholarship,
and education by publishing worldwide. Oxford is a registered trade mark of
Oxford University Press in the UK and in certain other countries

First published 2001
Revised edition 2007
This new edition 2017

British Library Cataloguing in Publication Data

Data available

ISBN: 978-0-19-275902-3

10 9 8 7 6 5 4 3 2 1

Paper used in the production of this book is a natural,
recyclable product made from wood grown in sustainable forests.
The manufacturing process conforms to the environmental
regulations of the country of origin.

Printed in China

Oxford OWL

For school
Discover eBooks, inspirational
resources, advice and support

For home
Helping your child's learning
with free eBooks, essential
tips and fun activities

www.oxfordowl.co.uk

We're going on a word hunt...
In the Town

forklift truck

guard

bandstand

truck

map

theatre

BENEDICT BLATHWAYT

OXFORD

UNIVERSITY PRESS

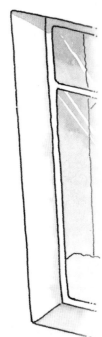

This is where we live

road

tunnel

bridge

reservoir

footpath

pavement

lamp post

flats

subway

flyover

runway

steps

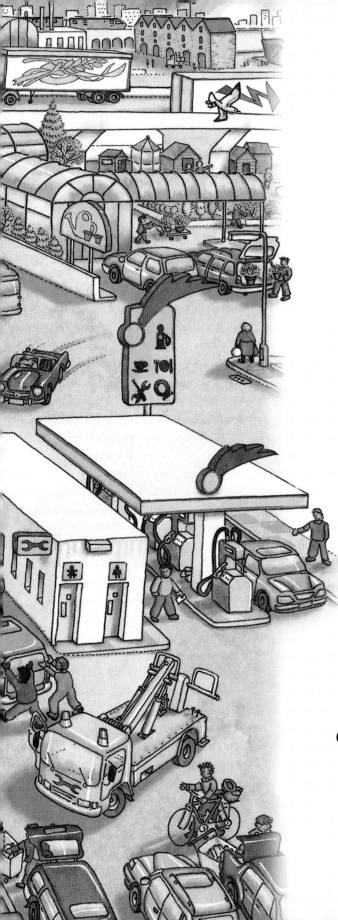

We are going shopping

bus stop

supermarket

garden centre

toilets

shopping trolley

garage

car park

shopping basket

petrol pump

cattle market

snack bar

delivery lorry

7

We are going on a journey

ticket

loudspeaker

timetable

clock

luggage trolley

map

suitcase

ticket machine

backpack

ticket office

guard

telephone

9

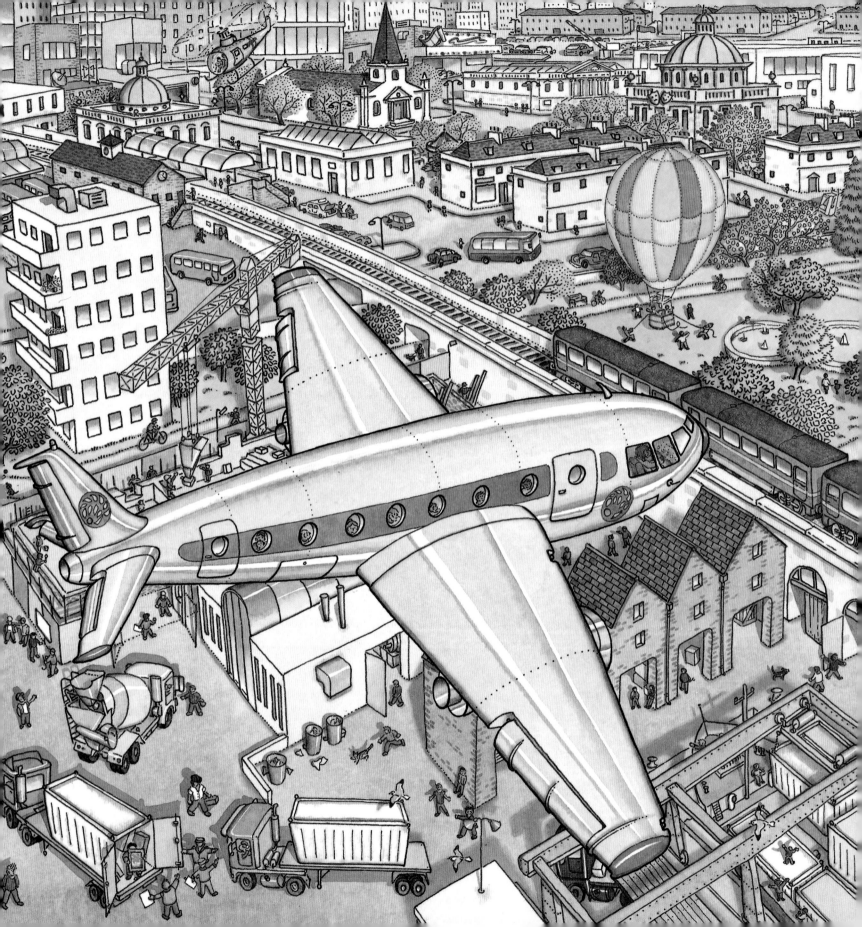

How we get around

bicycle

wheelchair

taxi

truck

train

balloon

motorbike

helicopter

boat

bus

car

aeroplane

Playing in the park

ball

litter bin

flower bed

bench

pushchair

pond

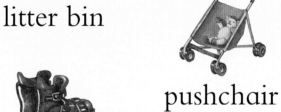

skates

slide

swings

sandpit

tree

skateboard

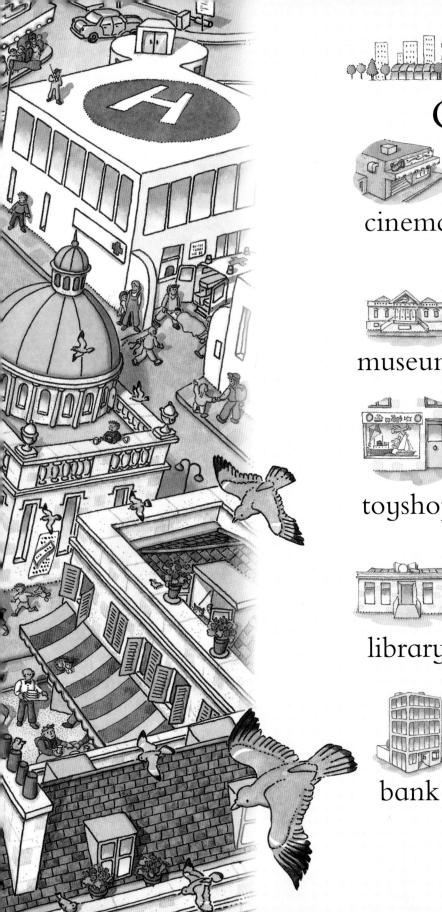

Our town centre

cinema

fire station

hospital

museum

restaurant

theatre

toyshop

bandstand

post office

library

police station

church

bank

market

Market day

stall

money

list

purse

shellfish

cakes

flowers

toys

fish

fruit

vegetables

bread

sparrows

boxes

Loading and unloading

crane

crate

container

conveyor

skip lorry

tipper truck

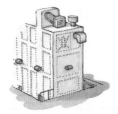
grain silo

barge

forklift truck

ship

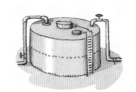
storage tank

fuel tanker

On the building site

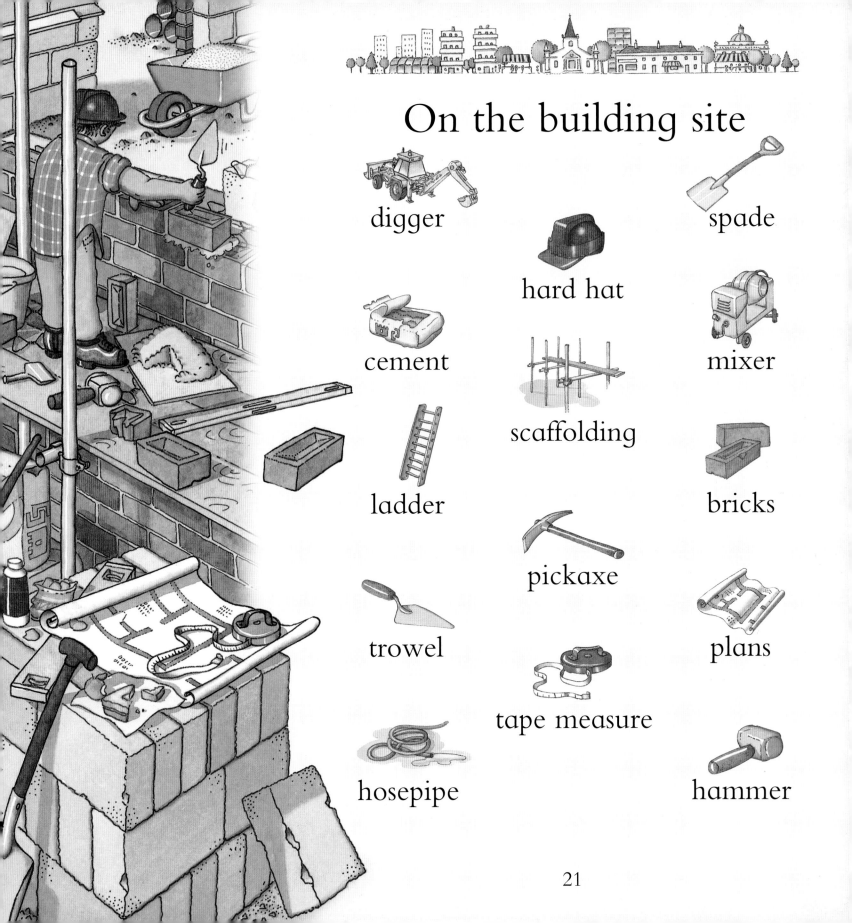

digger

spade

hard hat

cement

mixer

scaffolding

ladder

bricks

pickaxe

trowel

plans

tape measure

hosepipe

hammer

After school

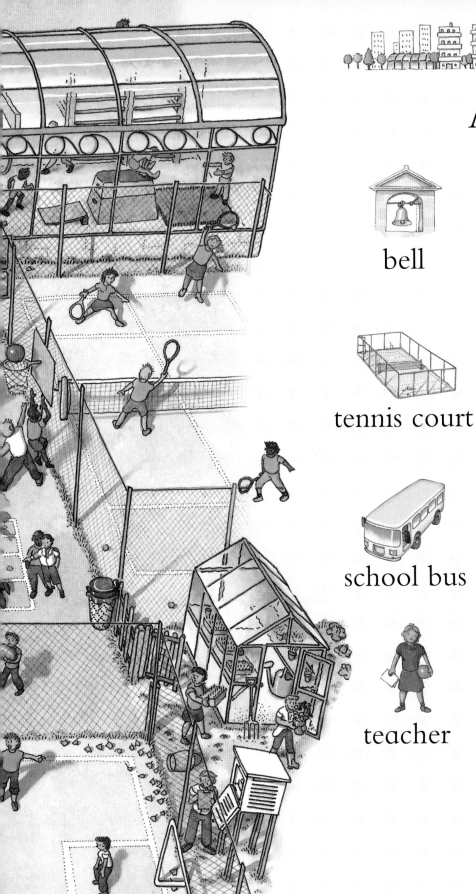

bell

playground

tennis court

recycling bin

gym

basketball net

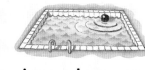

school bus

school bag

swimming pool

teacher

weather vane

football pitch

We're going on a word hunt
Can you match the words to the pictures?

(Answers are on the next page.)

digger

crane

playground

balloon

pond

flyover

car park

helicopter

football pitch

sandpit

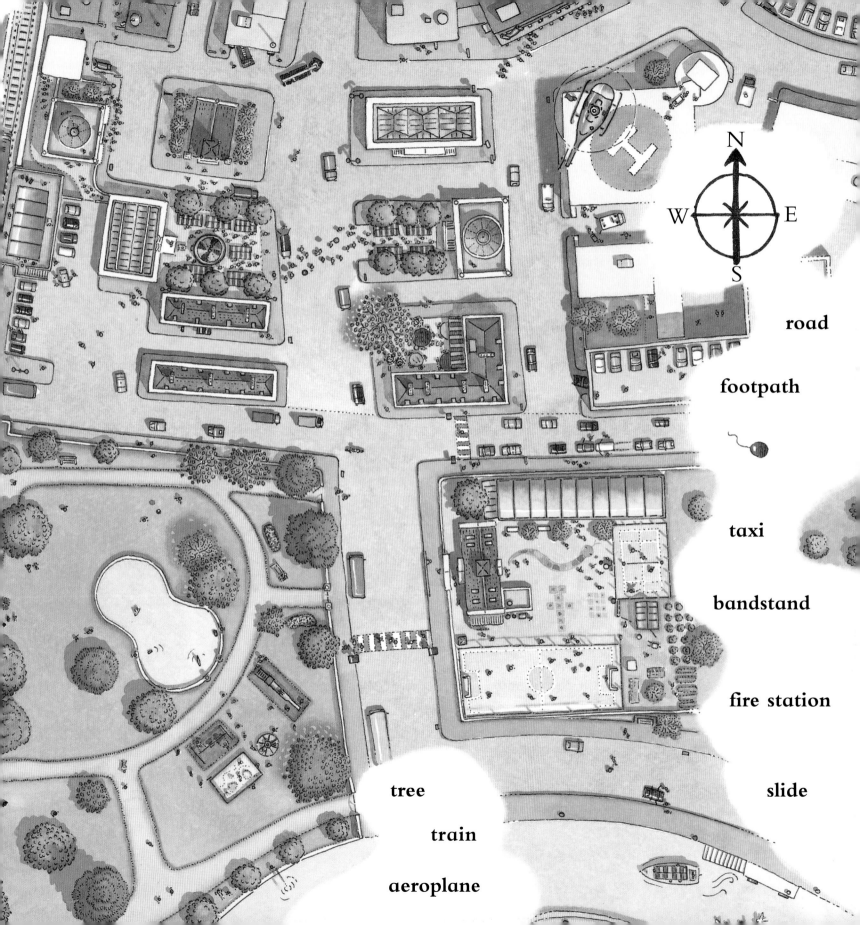

road

footpath

taxi

bandstand

fire station

tree

train

aeroplane

slide

N
W E
S

We're going on a word hunt
Can you match the words to the pictures?

(Answers)

flyover

road

digger

aeroplane

balloon

crane

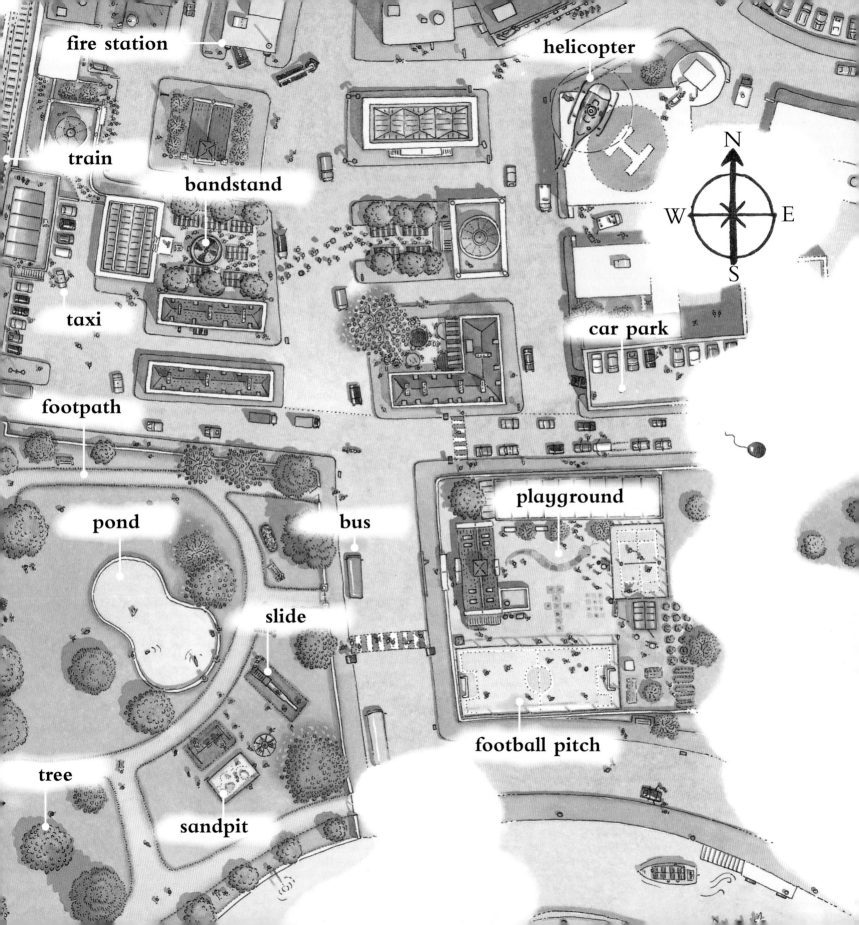

fire station

helicopter

train

bandstand

taxi

car park

footpath

playground

pond

bus

slide

football pitch

tree

sandpit

N
W   E
S

We're going on a word hunt
Can you find these words in the book?

(Look in the index to find the right page.)

Going for a walk

bridge   map   flower bed

backpack   reservoir

scaffolding

recycling bin

steps

Getting around

bus stop   ticket   ship

skates

pushchair

bicycle

school bus

car

Places to go

garden centre theatre library

supermarket swimming pool

tennis court stall bank

museum

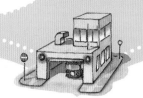

At work

teacher conveyor

restaurant cattle market garage

skip lorry post office

guard

Index

A

aeroplane 11

B

backpack 9
ball 13
balloon 11
bandstand 15
bank 15
barge 19
basketball net 23
bell 23
bench 13
bicycle 11
boat 11
boxes 17
bread 17
bricks 21
bridge 5
bus 11
bus stop 7

C

cakes 17
car 11
car park 7
cattle market 7
cement 21
church 15
cinema 15
clock 9
container 19
conveyor 19
crane 19
crate 19

D

delivery lorry 7
digger 21

F

fire station 15
fish 17
flats 5
flower bed 13
flowers 17
flyover 5
football pitch 23
footpath 5

forklift truck 19
fruit 17
fuel tanker 19

G

garage 7
garden centre 7
grain silo 19
guard 9
gym 23

H

hammer 21
hard hat 21
helicopter 11
hosepipe 21
hospital 15

L

ladder 21
lamp post 5
library 15
list 17
litter bin 13
loudspeaker 9
luggage trolley 9

M

map	9
market	15
mixer	21
money	17
motorbike	11
museum	15

P

pavement	5
petrol pump	7
pickaxe	21
plans	21
playground	23
police station	15
pond	13
post office	15
purse	17
pushchair	13

R

recycling bin	23
reservoir	5
restaurant	15
road	5
runway	5

S

sandpit	13
scaffolding	21
school bag	23
school bus	23
shellfish	17
ship	19
shopping basket	7
shopping trolley	7
skateboard	13
skates	13
skip lorry	19
slide	13
snack bar	7
spade	21
sparrows	17
stall	17
steps	5
storage tank	19
subway	5
suitcase	9
supermarket	7
swimming pool	23
swings	13

T

tape measure	21
taxi	11
teacher	23
telephone	9
tennis court	23
theatre	15
ticket	9
ticket machine	9
ticket office	9
timetable	9
tipper truck	19
toilets	7
toys	17
toyshop	15
train	11
tree	13
trowel	21
truck	11
tunnel	5

V

vegetables	17

W

weather vane	23
wheelchair	11

Other books you may enjoy:

Age 3+

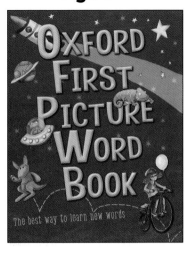

Age 4+

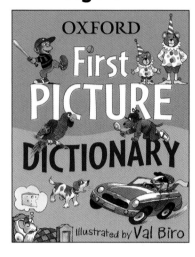

Age 4+

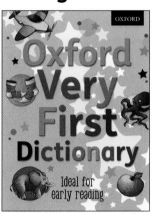

Age 5+

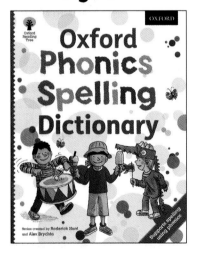

Age 5+

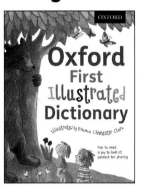

Age 5+

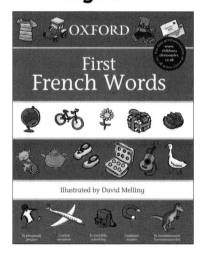

Age 5+

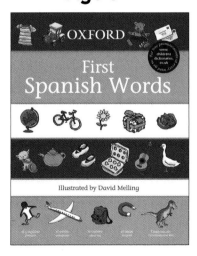